Little House, Little Town

Scott Beck

HARRY N. ABRAMS, INC., PUBLISHERS

For Reagan

Artist's Note

The illustrations for this book were made with acrylic paints on
Archer watercolor paper. After transferring the drawings with carbon
paper onto the watercolor paper, I paint in the larger areas with
very watery acrylic paint. Next, I paint the line work and fill in
the shapes, building up the color as necessary. Shadows and
small details are painted last.

Design: Becky Terhune
Production Manager: Jonathan Lopes

Library of Congress Cataloging-in-Publication Data

Beck, Scott.
Little house, little town / Scott Beck.
p. cm.
Summary: Evokes a gentle rhythm of life slowed down with a new baby.
ISBN 0-8109-4930-X (alk. paper)
[1. Babies—Fiction. 2. Day—Fiction. 3. Stories in rhyme.] I. Title.

PZ8.3.B38958Lit 2004
[E]—dc22
2004000874

Printed and bound in China
10 9 8 7 6 5 4 3 2 1

Harry N. Abrams, Inc.
100 Fifth Avenue
New York, NY 10011
www.abramsbooks.com

Abrams is a subsidiary of

LA MARTINIÈRE
GROUPE

In the little house, in the little town,

a baby wakes and Mama takes him in her arm.

Daddy gets a bottle warm.

Boys on bikes ride by.

A neighbor hangs her sheets to dry.

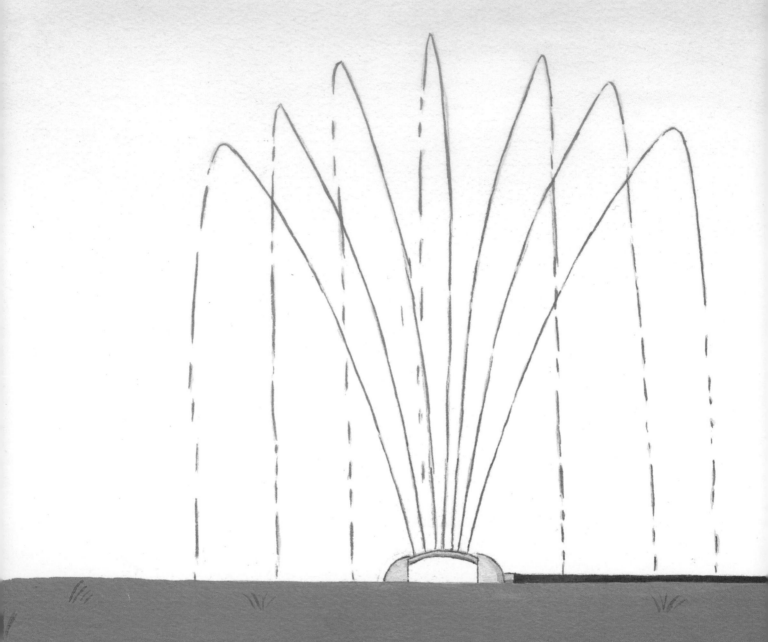

Daddy turns the sprinkler on.

Mama yawns a little yawn
and pats her baby's back.

Outside, the train goes down the track.

The mailman lifts his heavy sack.

The grocer puts a can on top.

Red light! Cars and buses stop.

Baby goes out for a walk
and listens to his parents talk.

Girls climb. Dogs bark.

People head home from the park.

The mechanic puts his tools away.

Children come in from their play.

Now it's getting dark.

Daddy rocks his boy to sleep.

And with a kiss upon the cheek,
he puts his baby down . . .

in his little crib,

in their little house,

in the little town.